Sleeping
Beauty

Illustrated by Richard Johnson

A king and queen had
a baby girl. The good
fairies came to see her.

"How beautiful she is!"
they said.

Aurora

Level 2 is ideal for children who have received some reading instruction and can read short, simple sentences with help.

Special features:

Frequent repetition of main story words and phrases

Short, simple sentences

The king and queen fell asleep, and everybody in the castle fell asleep.

Years went by and thorns grew on the castle.

20

Large, clear type

The prince cut down the thorns and went in the castle.

He looked at the sleeping princess.

"How beautiful she is!" he said.

Careful match between story and pictures

24

25

Educational Consultant: Geraldine Taylor
Book Banding Consultant: Kate Ruttle

A catalogue record for this book is available from the British Library

All correspondence to
Ladybird Books
Penguin Random House Children's Books
One Embassy Gardens, 8 Viaduct Gardens, London SW11 7BW

019
© LADYBIRD BOOKS LTD MMX. This edition MMXIII
Ladybird, Read It Yourself and the Ladybird Logo are registered or
unregistered trademarks of Ladybird Books Limited.

All rights reserved. No part of this publication may be reproduced,
stored in a retrieval system, or transmitted in any form or by any means,
electronic, mechanical, photocopying, recording or otherwise,
without the prior consent of the copyright owner.

ISBN: 978-0-72327-293-9

Printed in China

The fairies cast spells
for the baby princess.

"She will be kind,"
said one fairy.

"She will be clever,"
said another fairy.

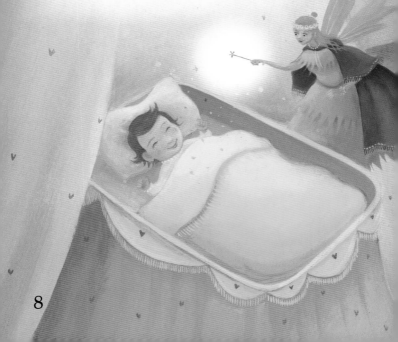

Then, a bad fairy came in.
She looked at the
baby princess.

"How beautiful she is!"
said the bad fairy.

Then she cast a bad spell.

"The princess will prick
her finger and die!"
she said.

13

But then a good fairy
cast a spell.
"The princess will not die.
She will prick her finger
and fall asleep for
one hundred years."

15

Years went by and the princess grew more kind and more beautiful.

One day, the princess
found a spinning wheel
and pricked her finger.

She fell asleep.

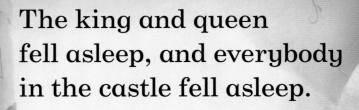

The king and queen
fell asleep, and everybody
in the castle fell asleep.

Years went by and thorns
grew on the castle.

One hundred years
went by.

Then one day, a prince
came to the castle.

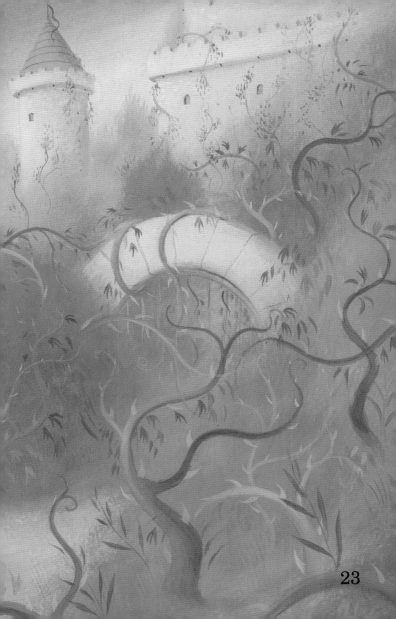

23

The prince cut down
the thorns and went
in the castle.

He looked at the
sleeping princess.

"How beautiful she is!"
he said.

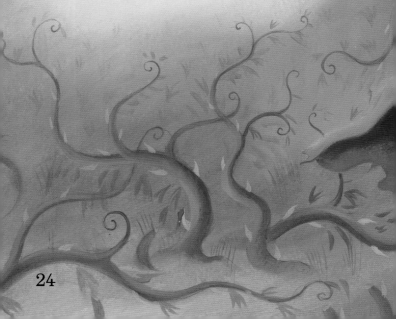

The prince gave the sleeping princess a kiss and she woke up.

The king and queen woke up, and everybody in the castle woke up, too.

"Will you marry me?"
said the prince.

"Yes," said the princess.
So she did!

How much do you remember about the story of Sleeping Beauty? Answer these questions and find out!

- What spell does the bad fairy cast?

- What does Sleeping Beauty prick her finger on?

- How long does everyone fall asleep for?

- How does the prince wake up Sleeping Beauty?